The Mourners' Bench

George Brant

A Samuel French Acting Edition

SAMUEL FRENCH

FOUNDED 1830

SAMUELFRENCH.COM
SAMUELFRENCH-LONDON.CO.UK

MUSIC USE NOTE

Licensees are solely responsible for obtaining formal written permission from copyright owners to use copyrighted music in the performance of this play and are strongly cautioned to do so. If no such permission is obtained by the licensee, then the licensee must use only original music that the licensee owns and controls. Licensees are solely responsible and liable for all music clearances and shall indemnify the copyright owners of the play(s) and their licensing agent, Samuel French, against any costs, expenses, losses and liabilities arising from the use of music by licensees. Please contact the appropriate music licensing authority in your territory for the rights to any incidental music.

IMPORTANT BILLING AND CREDIT REQUIREMENTS

If you have obtained performance rights to this title, please refer to your licensing agreement for important billing and credit requirements.

THE MOURNERS' BENCH was first produced by the Trinity Repertory Company, Curt Columbus, Artistic Director, Michael Gennaro, Executive Director, in 2012. The performance was directed by Michael Perlman, with sets by Michael McGarty, costumes by William Lane, lights by Dan Scully, and sound by Peter Sasha Hurowitz. The Production Stage Manager was Michael Domue. The cast was as follows:

MELISSA . . . . .Angela Brazil

BOBBY. . . . . .Mauro Hantman

WILMA. . . . . Janice Duclos

CAROLINE . . . . .Phyllis Kay

SARAH. . . . . .Anne Scurria

JOE . . . . Timothy Crowe

THE MOURNERS' BENCH was written while in residence at the WordBRIDGE Playwrights Laboratory and Blue Mountain Center. It received further developmental assistance from Naomi Wallace, Florida Studio Theatre, HRC Showcase Theatre, Djerassi Resident Artists Program, the Hangar Theatre Pilot Reading Series, and Trinity Repertory Company.

CHARACTERS

ACT ONE

MELISSA – early 30's, tightly wound, a survivor

BOBBY – two years younger than Melissa, alcoholic, childish, occasionally maudlin

ACT TWO

WILMA – mid-30's, a kind woman, feels everything deeply

CAROLINE – early 40's, direct force of nature, attractive in a severe way

ACT THREE

SARAH – late 40's - early 50's, deeply in love, glows despite ill health

JOE – 50's, deeply in love, generous, understanding

All pairs of characters share a common emotional language.

MUSIC

The same piece of piano music (Alberto Nepomuceno's "Prece" is strongly suggested) should be played throughout, ideally a piece with a strong melody, equal parts lovely and melancholy. How long and how well the piece is played in each instance is left to the director's discretion.

TIME

Use of projections or program notes to announce when each Act occurs (i.e. "Thirty years earlier…") is discouraged.

SPECIAL THANKS

Laura Kepley, The Brant/Kepley/Dumler/Jacobs/Alexander families, Dave White, Mark Charney, Will Manning, Kerrie Brown Seymour, Erik Ramsey, Stewart Olsen, David Kranes, Ben Strader, Maleea Acker, Mark Barr, Meera Subramanian, Alice Gordon, Lisa Iglesias, Mohan Sikka, Julia Oldham, Naomi Wallace, Amanda Cayo, Richard Hopkins, Kate Alexander, James Ashford, E.L. Keene, Barbara Wadlinger, Stephanie Yankwitt, Sanaz Ghajarrahimi, Stephen Berenson, Craig Watson, Curt Columbus, Michael Gennaro, Tyler Dobrowsky, Angela Brazil, Mauro Hantman, Janice Duclos, Phyllis Kay, Anne Scurria, Timothy Crowe, Michael Domue, and Michael Perlman.

For all I call Home

"How long, how long is the mourners' bench upon which we sit, arms linked in undeluded friendship, all of us, brief links, ourselves, in the eternal pity."

- *Blood of the Lamb,* Peter De Vries

ACT ONE

(A man and woman in a tastefully furnished, if out-of-date, suburban living room. A baby grand piano is the room's primary focus; it sits in a place of honor: up against the picture window looking out into the front yard. The man sits comfortably, the woman stands – nervous, confused and furious. A glass of water sits near her, a glass of scotch near him. A moment of silence, broken by –)

BOBBY. *(the piano)* Do you still play?

MELISSA. How could you do this?

BOBBY. I'd love it if you'd –

MELISSA. How?

BOBBY. …I had to.

MELISSA. Story of your life.

BOBBY. This is different.

MELISSA. You're right. It's worse.

*(**MELISSA** sprays her hands with sanitizer and rubs them together violently.)*

BOBBY. You don't have to do that.

MELISSA. I don't want to catch anything. Bring it home to the kids.

BOBBY. I'm not contagious.

MELISSA. Not you. It's in the air. They're in the air.

BOBBY. I know. Isn't it wonderful?

MELISSA. Have you been drinking?

BOBBY. Rhetorical.

MELISSA. Super. So we've moved beyond the debate, now.

BOBBY. I'm at peace with it. I've had five years – alone – to make peace with it.

(**MELISSA** *is wounded. Pause. She changes the subject.*)

MELISSA. They're the same color.

BOBBY. What?

MELISSA. The walls. They can't have kept the walls this color.

BOBBY. No, they papered over them. Salmon paisley.

MELISSA. So. You had them stripped, painted. Back to this.

BOBBY. Did it myself, actually.

MELISSA. When?

BOBBY. Week ago.

MELISSA. I'm surprised you didn't ask me over to help.

BOBBY. Thought about it.

MELISSA. But you wanted to save my visit till now. Wait till the walls were restored, the drapes cleaned. Wait till the museum was ready. Open for business.

BOBBY. It's not a museum.

MELISSA. No?

BOBBY. Museums are dead. This is alive.

MELISSA. It most certainly is not.

BOBBY. You said it yourself. They're in the air. Wanna see the back yard?

MELISSA. Not particularly.

BOBBY. There was this huge garden. It was actually kinda pretty, but –

MELISSA. You tore it up. Because we had grass.

BOBBY. Yep. How 'bout upstairs?

MELISSA. No thanks.

BOBBY. Our room. That one I really had to fix. The Callahans had –

MELISSA. Who?

BOBBY. The people who bought it after we moved.

MELISSA. Right.

BOBBY. No kids. They made it into an office or something. Our room. An office. The whole second floor was totally – it's not like down here, where it's all the same furniture and everything, I had to –

MELISSA. This is the room they kept the same?

BOBBY. It was nice stuff. And cheap. Part of the package.

MELISSA. But still. Freaks.

BOBBY. Hey.

I found our masterpiece up there.

MELISSA. What?

BOBBY. The one we made before we left. Drew in the back corner of our closet so the new owners wouldn't find it. It's still there.

(**MELISSA** *softens.*)

MELISSA. Not paisley'd over?

BOBBY. Nope.

MELISSA. *(smiling)* It worked.

BOBBY. It did. You were smart for eight.

MELISSA. No. Just lucky. They would've found it if they'd had kids. Kids would've found it.

BOBBY. Sure.

MELISSA. Can you imagine? If we'd found something like that? What mysteries we would've created?

BOBBY. Hieroglyphics from an earlier age.

MELISSA. Exactly. Those Callahan kids would've been the same, tried to decipher it. Break the code.

BOBBY. Wouldn't've been too hard – stick figures holding hands. Our initials.

MELISSA. No, they would've made it more complicated than that. We'd become legend.

BOBBY. No doubt.

MELISSA. What a waste! So many nooks for kids to explore. The tile floor in the kitchen! All those alternating colors – one gigantic game board. Mom's trying to make dinner and we're rolling dice and moving plastic soldiers between her feet.

BOBBY. Only time she'd get mad.

MELISSA. Kitchen floor must have been sorry to see us go. Not magic anymore, just a floor.

BOBBY. It's worse. They tore it up. The Callahans. Put in fake wood.

MELISSA. Of course they did. Childless creeps.

BOBBY. But I fixed it, found it, the tile, something close anyway, had to age it a little -

MELISSA. *(smiling)* Spill chocolate milk on it here and there –

BOBBY. Exactly, exactly.

(**MELISSA***'s smile fades.*)

What?

MELISSA. Don't get too excited, okay? This is a one-time visit. An exception. Then we're back to the rule.

BOBBY. Your rule.

MELISSA. That I will see you when you're sober.

BOBBY. This place will cure me.

MELISSA. Here?

BOBBY. It's kept me alive till now. A beacon, a comfort, to look through the window, to see…it's all that's kept me alive. Especially with you gone.

MELISSA. Bobby.

BOBBY. And now that I'm here, now that I'm actually back inside it - it will cure me.

MELISSA. Well, you can believe that if you want. If you need to. I can't, won't. You've dangled the sobriety carrot in front of me too many times.

BOBBY. You've really given up on me. Completely.

MELISSA. I have.

BOBBY. Was that…easy?

MELISSA. No.

BOBBY. Did you miss me?

MELISSA. Yes.

BOBBY. Five years.

MELISSA. Four and a half.

BOBBY. Five.

MELISSA. Four and a half.

BOBBY. Okay, okay.

How are the kids?

MELISSA. "The kids" are fine. Remember their names?

BOBBY. Melissa, come on.

MELISSA. I won't ask you to remember their birthdays, we won't get too complicated God forbid, but how 'bout their names?

BOBBY. Um…sure, she's… Violet.

MELISSA. Good.

BOBBY. And he's…

(A lost cause.)

MELISSA. …James.

BOBBY. …right. And they're…nine?

MELISSA. Six and eight.

BOBBY. Six and eight?

MELISSA. Six and eight.

BOBBY. That's the same age as we –

MELISSA. I know. Do you think I don't know? How could I not know?

(Beat.)

BOBBY. And Brian?

MELISSA. Brian's fine.

BOBBY. He always seemed like a nice guy.

MELISSA. He is.

BOBBY. And he treats you – ?

MELISSA. He loves me. Yes.

BOBBY. I'm – I'm glad it's worked out for you. I think of… when I can see through the fog of jealousy, I – I think of you, see you at your home, gathered 'round the spinet singing Christmas carols, being perfect. I'm glad it's worked out.

MELISSA. Thank you.

How 'bout you? Any surprises? Kids I don't know about?

BOBBY. No.

MELISSA. Kids you don't know about?

BOBBY. *(laughing)* Maybe.

(Beat.)

MELISSA. Why did you do this?

BOBBY. I had to.

Everything aligned.

MELISSA. What?

BOBBY. *(excited)* Okay. So, I was randomly driving by the house a month ago –

MELISSA. Driving by? Why would you – ?

BOBBY. Exactly. So. I'm randomly driving by, late at night, I see an ambulance out front.

MELISSA. Oh my God.

BOBBY. I know, I know, intense. Bought a paper the next day, saw the obituary for Mr. Callahan. It was like he wanted me to have it.

MELISSA. What?

BOBBY. A gift. Checked the listings, waiting, hoping. It was on the market within the week.

MELISSA. That doesn't –

BOBBY. And the kicker? The asking price? Exactly what I had left.

MELISSA. What?

BOBBY. Exactly. Everything I had left in the trust.

MELISSA. I hope you're kidding.

BOBBY. Almost to the penny. You see? It all aligned!

MELISSA. It all – ? How are you going to live? Eat?

BOBBY. Doesn't matter.

MELISSA. For Christ's sake, do I have to hold your hand forever?

BOBBY. Don't flatter yourself. You gave that up a while back. Four and a half years back.

MELISSA. Out of necessity. Self-preservation.

BOBBY. Well, this was necessity, too.

(Beat. Shift.)

It was crazy, walking in here again. I almost called you when I pulled up to meet the realtor, asked you if -

MELISSA. I wouldn't have come.

BOBBY. I know. So I just stood there alone in the doorway, shaking. I'd seen it plenty of times from the outside, but –

MELISSA. Randomly driving by?

BOBBY. Right. But this was…

That salmon paper. I almost screamed, almost scratched it off the walls with my fingernails. Same furniture, same piano, but that paper, that ugly fucking paper –

And then I went upstairs, to our room. And it just got worse. No tiny beds, no fish stencils around the ceiling border. Just some shitty metal desk and an exercise bike. I couldn't breathe, couldn't – I wanted to jump out the window, get out, out.

But then I saw the door, our bedroom door. The inside of it. I saw the scratches I'd made, I saw me. And I knew I had to have it. That it was mine, that I could make it mine again. That I could set it right.

MELISSA. Set it right? By laying tile?

BOBBY. I should've grown up here. I should have shaved in the sink. I should've snuck girls in through the windows. I should've taken a picture of you coming down the stairs on the way to prom.

MELISSA. All those things happened.

BOBBY. But not here. They were supposed to happen here.

MELISSA. Get a grip.

BOBBY. I have.

MELISSA. At some point you've got to – I've lived a life, okay? I've made that choice.

BOBBY. Here we go.

MELISSA. You've been stuck in this, this limbo. You have to grow up.

BOBBY. I bought a house. That isn't growing up?

MELISSA. You didn't buy a house.

BOBBY. Pretty sure I did.

MELISSA. Not really.

BOBBY. I bought it!

MELISSA. Yeah? With whose money?

(Pause.)

Mom and Dad. Mom and Dad bought you this house.

BOBBY. Good. They should have.

MELISSA. Not a dime of your own.

BOBBY. They owed it to me. For taking it away in the first place.

MELISSA. They didn't – Mom didn't.

BOBBY. No.

She didn't.

Do you still play?

MELISSA. Sometimes, yes.

BOBBY. That's good. You're lucky.

MELISSA. Am I?

BOBBY. I couldn't sit still, I wouldn't sit.

MELISSA. James won't either.

BOBBY. Always had to be riding that stupid bike. Why wouldn't I let her teach me? Why couldn't I settle the fuck down? Just focus! Focus!

MELISSA. You were young.

BOBBY. But you teach your kids, right?, you teach…uh…

MELISSA. …Violet.

BOBBY. Yeah, you teach her. She can sit still.

MELISSA. So what? So you couldn't.

BOBBY. I know, but – if I – I'd have something. A comfort, something more. You have something more. I have pictures in my head of her, but that…they fade, you know? They fade. Sometimes I…I don't feel her at all. I try to get her back, squeeze my eyes shut until my head throbs, but sometimes I just…I can't find her. But you – you have…you have her in your bones, your fingers. She gave you every note you play, every motion that makes the chords. She's inside you.

MELISSA. That's not always easy.

BOBBY. Don't say that. It's a gift. If I had that inside me? That love, that joy? I could do anything with that love.

MELISSA. It helps.

BOBBY. What do I have inside of me?

MELISSA. Drink.

BOBBY. That's not her.

MELISSA. I didn't say it was.

BOBBY. I think about that. I'm not stupid, I…I do.

MELISSA. You should. You should think about it a lot.

BOBBY. Would you play something for me?

MELISSA. Bobby.

BOBBY. Something she used to?

MELISSA. That's not a good idea.

BOBBY. It would mean the world.

MELISSA. I don't have the music.

(**BOBBY** *smiles. He opens the piano bench. It's full of sheet music.*)

That, too?

BOBBY. It had to be perfect. Most of it was still in there, the rest I tracked down…what I could remember.

(**MELISSA** *is disturbed but touched. She picks out a book of music and sits on the piano bench. She lifts the fall, and lowers her fingers on to the keys. As she does so, her face settles a bit, calms. She caresses the keys for a moment without making a sound.*)

She's there, isn't she?

MELISSA. Yes.

(**MELISSA** *plays the piano piece. Her playing begins hesitantly, but blossoms into something beautiful – not the work of a concert pianist, but lovely, nonetheless.* **BOBBY** *closes his eyes, beyond ecstasy. After a moment, he stands and begins to dance along to the music, like a child, his movement full of twirls and leaps and awkward gestures.* **MELISSA** *notices him, but does not stop. Both are in tune with their mother and their younger selves, caught in a trance. The piece concludes on a gentle, hushed note. The reverberation of the last keys struck fills the room as they stare at each other.*)

MELISSA. They do that, too. My kids.

BOBBY. Must be in the genes. *(smiling)* Are they as graceful?

MELISSA. They're getting there.

BOBBY. Bless you, God bless you. You fill your house with it. Like she did. Music. Thick in the air. Drifting up the stairs, down into the basement. Whatever game we were playing, whatever we were doing, she was always there in the air, accompanying us, surrounding us. The music was always there.

MELISSA. Until it stopped.

BOBBY. Yes.

(*She lowers the fall.*)

MELISSA. I should go.

BOBBY. No.

MELISSA. Listen. Now that I've got my own – she should've left him. Called Aunt Wilma or Caroline. Grabbed us. Stolen out in the middle of the night.

BOBBY. When?

MELISSA. Whenever! It doesn't matter.

BOBBY. He would've found us.

MELISSA. Are you kidding? He wouldn't have noticed for weeks. Holed up in his lair, the Shush Room, walled in with his bottles of scotch and books.

BOBBY. She couldn't just – you don't just –

MELISSA. Escape?

BOBBY. It's not that easy. The, the, the weight, the pull of this place, can't you feel it?

MELISSA. Bobby –

BOBBY. The gravitational – it's where we belong. You aren't meant to leave me anymore, you're meant to be by my side.

MELISSA. To do what? Watch you drink yourself to death? You don't need another person to kill yourself.

BOBBY. That's not what we were taught.

MELISSA. FUCK YOU.

BOBBY. Missy –

(**MELISSA** *grabs her things and moves toward the door. Trying to stop her,* **BOBBY** *grabs her arm more violently than he intends.* **MELISSA** *responds to his affront furiously, striking the repentant* **BOBBY** *viciously and shoving him to the floor.*)

MELISSA. You don't get to touch me. Do you understand? Don't ever touch me again.

BOBBY. I'm sorry, I'm – please. Just stay. For a little longer.

MELISSA. Tell you what, a deal. I'll stay if you can tell me something new. Anything. Anything new. Do you have anything new to tell me?

BOBBY. What?

MELISSA. Since I last saw you. And I'll stay. That's five years. Surprise me. Surprise me! Something new, some progression of some kind, on any level, any level at all and I'll stay.

Want me to go first? I could tell you fifteen new things
that happened to me just today. Fifteen. I have lived
a life, Bobby. I have walked out from underneath the
shadow of this house. I have gone to college, I have
made friends, I have allowed someone to love me, I
have had children with him. I have made a million
mistakes and had a million triumphs. I am a person. I
am not a broken record. Give me something new!

BOBBY. I'm your brother.

MELISSA. Heard that one before.

BOBBY. You have to help me.

MELISSA. Heard it.

BOBBY. You can't leave me.

MELISSA. Heard it.

BOBBY. You fucking cunt!

MELISSA. A classic. And with that –

(She motions to leave.)

BOBBY. Wait, wait, I have new! I have new!

MELISSA. Let's hear it!

BOBBY. A surprise!

MELISSA. What? What, Bobby? What's your surprise?

BOBBY. I bought this for you!

(Quiet.)

MELISSA. That better not be true.

BOBBY. It is. And I surprised you. So now you have to stay.

MELISSA. No.

BOBBY. That was the deal, your deal.

MELISSA. You used all your money to – ?

BOBBY. It worked.

MELISSA. There are cheaper ways to get my attention. You
don't buy a fucking house to –

BOBBY. It worked, though. I can see you. I can *(the piano)*
hear you. I can touch you.

MELISSA. And now what? We play house? I have a husband, children.

BOBBY. Right, your family, your do-over.

MELISSA. Shut up.

BOBBY. Your do-over without me. You can't wait to cut me out of the family portrait, make it perfect.

MELISSA. That's not true.

BOBBY. A pair of scissors at my funeral.

MELISSA. What are you – ?

BOBBY. Snip!

MELISSA. Shut up.

BOBBY. Snip as they lower me down: "Thank God I don't have to worry about him any more, don't have to worry about how he's doing, where he is – "

MELISSA. Stop it.

BOBBY. And you'll finally have a simple answer. When all your million fucking million friends ask you about your brother, you won't have to answer "I don't know" ever again. You'll have a new answer, a simple one, one that doesn't sound so bad, one that doesn't sound like you abandoned me, failed me. A new answer: "Him? Oh, he's dead."

MELISSA. That's not what I want.

BOBBY. "He's dead."

MELISSA. I have two kids who need me.

BOBBY. Fuck your kids.

MELISSA. Watch it.

BOBBY. They are nothing! Please, kids, a husband? What are they?

MELISSA. I love them.

BOBBY. You should love me more!

MELISSA. I don't.

BOBBY. You have to! After what we went through! You have to!

MELISSA. I don't.

BOBBY. *(losing it completely)* You held my hand! You held my hand!

MELISSA. I know, I –

BOBBY. You held my hand!

(**BOBBY** *collapses, childlike, in a heap on the floor. Quiet. Pity creeps into* **MELISSA***'s eyes. A shift.*)

MELISSA. You're right.

I do love you more.

They enter my heart but only so far. You were there early enough, before the layers of shame and loss and confusion, before all that calcified around the core. You got there first. You're at the core of my heart, Bobby.

But it hurts. Those layers trap you in as much as they keep others out. And you've grown – you're not six anymore. You hurt me, my heart, press against it from the inside, a grown man trapped in the space of a child.

BOBBY. I don't have to be grown. Not here. I could play our games, I could dance, I could dance for you all day long.

MELISSA. Bobby.

BOBBY. Why not? Can't leave your perfect home?

MELISSA. It's not perfect.

I don't live there right now.

Temporary.

I hope.

Brian's doing.

BOBBY. Did he hurt you?

MELISSA. *(small laugh)* Brian? No. I made sure I picked someone who could never...he'd never do that. I married a man who loved me – that was first on my list – really loved me, but that proved harder to deal with than I…harder to accept…as true. But, no. It wasn't him.

It was the kids.

BOBBY. *(disbelieving)* They're beautiful.

MELISSA. They are.

But I needed more of them.

More than two. More than a boy and a girl. I couldn't have just the two. It needed to be different than here. I needed to do it different.

BOBBY. Missy.

MELISSA. The last four years…I kept trying for more but they kept…so much blood… Brian couldn't take it anymore, stopped having sex with me, hoped I wouldn't notice. But I'd grab him in the middle of the night, stroke him awake, force myself on him.

Rape him. Rape my husband.

It didn't matter.

They died all the same.

The doctor told me to stop trying, that it could kill me.

Just words.

Last week I attacked Brian again…and he threw me out of bed. Packed me a bag.

I'm supposed to think about things for a while.

BOBBY. Where are you staying?

MELISSA. Hotel.

BOBBY. Not anymore. You're here, you're home.

MELISSA. This isn't home. It can't be.

It's not just her. The moment I walked in the door I started breathing differently. My lungs remembered: this is what you do here. Careful, shallow, shallow, don't disturb Daddy. Daddy's working, Daddy's reading, reading.

All those books. That door, closed, locked. A room full of books, and he couldn't read us one.

BOBBY. No.

MELISSA. I read to James and Vi every night. Every fucking night. Whether they want to or not. Book after book after book.

BOBBY. Good.

MELISSA. Long after they've fallen asleep. Fill their dreams with books, with me. Why didn't he love us?

BOBBY. I don't know.

MELISSA. Brian loves them, he'd do anything to protect them.

Even kick me out.

(**BOBBY** *has no reply.*)

What were we playing?

BOBBY. What?

MELISSA. Before he did it.

BOBBY. I don't know.

MELISSA. You know. You remembered the sheet music. You know.

BOBBY. …Uno.

MELISSA. Yes.

BOBBY. We were in our room playing Uno and he appeared in the doorway, staring at us. And we stared back, waiting.

MELISSA. Yes.

BOBBY. And then we saw the gun.

MELISSA. Yes.

BOBBY. And then we waited.

MELISSA. Yes.

BOBBY. And then he went downstairs.

MELISSA. Yes.

BOBBY. And then we heard the sound.

MELISSA. Yes.

BOBBY. And then the music stopped.

MELISSA. Yes.

BOBBY. And then we heard the sound again.

MELISSA. Yes.

BOBBY. And then you locked me in our room and then you went downstairs.

MELISSA. Yes.

BOBBY. And then you screamed.

MELISSA. Yes.

BOBBY. You screamed.

MELISSA. Yes.

BOBBY. And then I tried to get out, I scratched and scratched and scratched and scratched and scratched… You should've let me see them.

MELISSA. I spared you.

BOBBY. Denied me.

MELISSA. Don't say that. They were…and the walls were…

BOBBY. I imagined worse. I'm sure I imagined worse.

MELISSA. No.

You didn't.

Why the house, Bobby?

BOBBY. To cure me. Us.

I bought a gun. His gun. Same kind.

It's in the piano bench. Under the music.

I wanted… I wanted you to come and… I thought we could…we could finish it.

MELISSA. Finish – ?

BOBBY. What they started. Here. In this house. We could end it. End the curse. I think it's what we're meant to do.

MELISSA. He was a sick man.

BOBBY. So am I. So are we.

MELISSA. No.

BOBBY. What do you have? Really? What did they leave us with?

MELISSA. Love. She, at least. You were right, I can feel it, when I play.

BOBBY. I can't. She's gone. Her, her love. He killed it.

MELISSA. Don't say that.

BOBBY. We're lost.

MELISSA. No.

BOBBY. Tell me you're not lost. Tell me that. Tell me and I'll stop. I'll shut up. Tell me. Please tell me.

(No reply.)

What are the fifteen things you've done today? Huh? That make you better than me. Your turn. Yours now. Name one. Just one. One.

We could end it, Melissa. All the shame, emptiness, nightmares. End it. We just have to decide who goes first.

*(A moment. **MELISSA** rises. She walks slowly to the piano bench. She opens it. She reaches in, perhaps pulls out the gun, stops. She places the gun back, closes the bench and sits.)*

BOBBY. Missy.

Please.

*(**MELISSA** lifts the fall.)*

Please. I can't –

MELISSA. Quiet.

I'll teach you.

BOBBY. What?

MELISSA. I'll teach you.

(A pause. He rises. He walks toward her slowly, joins her on the bench.)

Here.

(She starts to move his hand toward the keys. He succumbs at first but then pulls back.)

BOBBY. Later.

Just play.

(She plays the piano piece. He places his hands on hers as she plays and closes his eyes. Lights fade to black.)

ACT TWO

*(Living room, as before, save for a section of the wall behind the piano, which is covered by a bed sheet or a cloth tarp. The sheet music from the previous act remains on the piano. A kind-looking, soft-spoken woman in her mid-30's, **WILMA**, and **CAROLINE**, a more attractive, but slightly severe woman in her early 40's. **WILMA** is dressed plainly, **CAROLINE** in more of an outfit. They stare at the piano.)*

CAROLINE. While she was playing? You're sure?

WILMA. Yes.

CAROLINE. How do you know?

WILMA. The children.

And the music.

CAROLINE. Sorry?

WILMA. The sheet music. It was still there. When the police came.

*(**CAROLINE** looks at the music on the piano.)*

CAROLINE. God.

WILMA. I taught her how to play that.

CAROLINE. And I taught you.

WILMA. On that tiny spinet.

CAROLINE. So this… *(the room)* is everything as it – ?

WILMA. Oh no, it was… *(can't find the words)* it's been cleaned, a service.

CAROLINE. *(the covered section of wall)* What about that?

WILMA. They said it's…stubborn. We may have to re-paint or –

CAROLINE. Of course.

(CAROLINE takes it in.)

God.

Right here. You have been a trouper.

WILMA. Not at all.

CAROLINE. You have been a trouper. Spending so much time here – just walking in the room must –

WILMA. Oh, I don't mind. I come here…a lot, actually. Even when I'm not showing the house.

CAROLINE. You're kidding.

WILMA. No. Every day, really. The afternoons. It's a comfort.

CAROLINE. A comfort.

WILMA. I didn't get to say goodbye.

CAROLINE. *(a bit annoyed)* You're not the only one.

WILMA. I know, but… I feel Evelyn here. More than at her grave, even. I'll be sorry when this room…when it's denied me.

CAROLINE. It's for the best.

WILMA. Yes, but couldn't we – you don't think there's a way we could hold on to it? I'd be happy to look after it, maintain it –

CAROLINE. Stop.

It's hard enough to make these decisions once. The money from the house goes into the trust for the children.

WILMA. Yes, of course. It'll…it'll be a comfort to them when they get older.

CAROLINE. Exactly. And God knows they need some of that.

How are they?

WILMA. Melissa's voice has changed – you'll hear, it's deeper. Only when she talks to him. Like she's playing at mother. She sounds…she sounds like Evelyn.

CAROLINE. And him?

WILMA. His problems are more…he keeps…going to the bathroom in his pants. Things like that.

CAROLINE. God.

You have been a trouper.

WILMA. I've tried. I've done my best.

CAROLINE. Of course you have.

So. Are they ready?

WILMA. Ready?

CAROLINE. Packed?

WILMA. I'm not sure.

CAROLINE. Wilma. This is horrible, this is horrible, this is horrible, but we've got to get through it, force ourselves. We've got to gallop through this and save the grieving for later.

WILMA. I know, but –

CAROLINE. We can't spend all day wading through the tar of this.

WILMA. Caroline, I've been here, I've lived it, I'm entitled to wade. I handled the funeral, the children, the, the cleaning –

CAROLINE. And I appreciate it –

WILMA. – showing the house, letting strangers walk in here, strangers, catching glances between them as they examine the scene of the crime, hoping to find a stray hair they can tell their friends about at a party.

CAROLINE. I'm sure that's not –

WILMA. They're vultures, I lead flocks of vultures through our sister's home.

CAROLINE. Then let's get an agent. Or stop showing for a while. It'll probably be months, years before anybody actually makes an offer. Even at a bargain.

WILMA. There was one gentleman.

Wednesday.

CAROLINE. And he might be serious?

WILMA. I think so.

CAROLINE. Is he from around here?

WILMA. A couple towns over.

CAROLINE. And did he know what... *(happened)*?

WILMA. Well.

I told him.

CAROLINE. Wilma! Oh, Jesus! Why would you – ?

WILMA. He couldn't understand why the price was so low.

CAROLINE. But you didn't have to volunteer – !

WILMA. He was such a kind man. It wouldn't have been fair to trick someone like that, it would've kept me up nights.

CAROLINE. And having this around our necks won't?

WILMA. It was the right thing to do. Besides, he – he didn't care.

CAROLINE. What?

WILMA. He thought about it and he nodded his head and he said it didn't matter. He said it was still perfect.

CAROLINE. Perfect? This?

WILMA. Perfect.

CAROLINE. And he's serious, you think he might actually be – ?

WILMA. He made an offer.

CAROLINE. He – ? Wilma! *(embracing her)* Wilma! Praise God! You did it!

WILMA. I haven't told him yes yet.

CAROLINE. Well then, tell him, tell him! Tell him before the weirdo changes his mind! You did it honey, you did it!

WILMA. It's just...he had conditions.

CAROLINE. What do you mean?

WILMA. The room, this room. He wants everything.

CAROLINE. The furniture? Good. Throw it in. Less to worry about.

WILMA. The piano. He wants the piano.

CAROLINE. And?

WILMA. The piano, Caroline. Her piano.

CAROLINE. Wilma. Give the man the piano. We won't see another offer for –

WILMA. I've always loved this piano. It would be a comfort – to have something of hers.

CAROLINE. Don't you screw this up, Wilma! Don't you do it!

WILMA. He might not have been serious.

CAROLINE. Give me his number. His phone.

WILMA. Why?

CAROLINE. I'll call him when I get back to the hotel. We'll settle this before I leave.

WILMA. I just wonder if –

CAROLINE. No. You need a push, let me be the push, I'm happy to be the push. I'll be the bad guy and you'll hate me until you see I'm right.

WILMA. I'll give it to you later.

CAROLINE. Okay, but I won't forget.

WILMA. I know. I'll give it to you.

CAROLINE. Yes, you will.

(Beat.)

WILMA. Mr. Callahan, the buyer…he didn't mention the upstairs.

CAROLINE. What about it?

WILMA. Wanting anything.

CAROLINE. Good taste.

WILMA. What…what do we do with his things?

CAROLINE. Whose?

WILMA. Oliver's. His study up there – an awful lot of books. There's twenty on his desk alone. Bring them to the library?

CAROLINE. They wouldn't take them.

WILMA. Maybe a different branch would –

CAROLINE. Burn them, we should burn them all. Crack their spines and roast them. The only satisfaction we'll get.

WILMA. Oh, Caroline, you're not –

CAROLINE. We can do it in the backyard. Start a bonfire on the lawn and throw them in from the windows. All his first editions, rarities, every precious volume soaring into the inferno.

WILMA. You're serious.

CAROLINE. Right before my flight. I'll carry the memory of those flames all the way back to Arizona. Kids'll keep asking why I've got a grin on my face. Well? What do you think?

WILMA. ...all right.

CAROLINE. You mean it?

WILMA. I'd like to find a way to punish him. Hurt him.

CAROLINE. Why, Wilma. You might just be human after all.

WILMA. Of course I'm human.

CAROLINE. I'm never sure. There's always been a whiff of the saint about you.

WILMA. *(smiling)* Now.

CAROLINE. It's kept you single.

WILMA. You know, it's silly but, I... I thought of myself as a saint when I was younger. Evelyn's patron saint.

CAROLINE. Really? I felt that way about you.

WILMA. You did?

CAROLINE. Well, I was maybe more your headmistress. Next to you on the bench, telling you to sit up straight.

WILMA. "Straighter, straighter!"

CAROLINE. I was probably dreadful.

WILMA. No, I did the same to her. More gentle encouragement, though, less rapping of knuckles.

CAROLINE. No! I didn't, did I?

WILMA. Maybe once or twice.

CAROLINE. Oh my God, I'm sorry, that's unforgivable.

WILMA. Not very hard. Just a tap, really.

CAROLINE. There's that saint again.

WILMA. But it worked. And I was able to pass it on.

(**WILMA** *caresses the piano for a moment.*)

I'm glad it… I'm glad it was here. I like to think that… at least…she was doing something she loved.

CAROLINE. Yes.

WILMA. She wasn't washing the dishes, she was…playing.

CAROLINE. Your song.

WILMA. *(the three of them)* Our song.

(*They share a smile.*)

I hope she never looked up.

CAROLINE. Or was looking out the window.

WILMA. I hope she was lost in the music.

CAROLINE. I hope she'd had a cocktail, had a warm glow.

WILMA. I hope she was thinking of the children.

CAROLINE. I hope she was at peace.

WILMA. I hope she felt me with her, in the song.

(*Beat.*)

I'm sorry, that's selfish.

CAROLINE. No.

Me, too.

(*Beat.*)

You two…did you talk…often?

WILMA. Not really. Once a day.

CAROLINE. Oh. Uh-huh.

WILMA. You?

CAROLINE. Not quite as much as that. Long distance.

WILMA. Yes it is. Very.

CAROLINE. Honey, I'm sorry that… I couldn't get away until now.

WILMA. I know.

CAROLINE. I don't want you to think that my opening was more important, or – there were debates with myself, long debates, Tom can tell you, I soul-searched for days, but when it came down to it, I realized, "what would Evelyn want? Would she want me to throw away all the work of the past year? All those countless hours?" And I swear I heard her, I heard her very clearly, she told me, "no. The gallery is your life now, Caroline. Come when you can. I'm not going anywhere."

WILMA. *(slight edge)* She gave you absolution.

CAROLINE. Better. She told me I didn't need it.

WILMA. A generous soul.

…it was a lovely funeral.

CAROLINE. The program was just beautiful. Thank you for sending it.

WILMA. One of her students typed it up. There were lots of them there. The church was full. It was…very heartening to see how many people cared.

CAROLINE. I'm sure.

How did the kids…?

WILMA. They held hands throughout the service, the burial, wouldn't let go. They still do. Sleeping together in my guest room, holding hands.

CAROLINE. You let them? The same bed?

WILMA. I'm hardly going to break them apart.

CAROLINE. Well, they'll have their own rooms at my house. Healthier.

WILMA. Oh no, Caroline, they need each other. Don't - !

CAROLINE. For a few weeks, maybe. But they have to gallop through this too.

WILMA. You must be gentle.

CAROLINE. That's not how you raise a child, honey. Tom and I have been through this. Parameters. Gentleness comes later.

WILMA. I'm not sure you realize what these two have been –

CAROLINE. Holding hands at the funeral is fine, but they can't do it the rest of their lives.

WILMA. Caroline –

CAROLINE. Trust me honey, you wouldn't understand.

(WILMA *backs down.*)

So, what about the bastard?

WILMA. What?

CAROLINE. His family. What did they do?

WILMA. Oh, it was a small service. Just immediate.

CAROLINE. I'm surprised they found a funeral home that was willing.

WILMA. I don't know if they're allowed to refuse.

CAROLINE. Probably not. I like that thought, though – Oliver driven from home to home, forced to wander the earth forever, slowly rotting away in the back seat of a station wagon.

WILMA. Well. Someone took him in.

CAROLINE. But it wasn't like hers.

WILMA. No.

CAROLINE. His was just a tape recording of an organ and five people with dry eyes. Hers was hundreds, hers was hundreds of souls ushering her into heaven.

WILMA. Yes.

…you should have been there.

CAROLINE. Hon.

WILMA. I felt so alone, lost… I could have used some of your confidence.

CAROLINE. I was there. In spirit. I was there. You must have felt me there.

WILMA. I felt nothing.

Just Evelyn in front of me and her children at my side.

(*A moment.*)

CAROLINE. Well.

We should get them packed.

WILMA. I'm keeping them.

(Quiet.)

CAROLINE. This has been decided. This has been discussed. This is why I flew out here.

WILMA. Oh, yes, because otherwise you couldn't have been bothered to –

CAROLINE. That is not what I meant.

WILMA. I'm keeping them.

CAROLINE. I have three plane tickets that say differently.

WILMA. I'll pay you back.

CAROLINE. And how will you do that? Wilma. Please.

WILMA. I'll find a way. For all of it. I've talked to my supervisor at work, he's willing to make adjustments in my schedule, I'll be able to drop them off at school, pick them up, he understood, was more than happy.

CAROLINE. You've thought this all out. Amassed your arguments.

WILMA. They like me. We're a family.

CAROLINE. This isn't how you get a family.

WILMA. I'm not saying – !

CAROLINE. By coveting your sister's –

WILMA. I never once – !?

CAROLINE. Of course not. Not the saint. You never once walked over here, stared in the window, wondered why it wasn't you sitting at the head of the table with your two perfect kids and your handsome husband.

WILMA. I was happy for her.

CAROLINE. You were. And that shows how much your judgement is worth.

*(**WILMA** is stunned, furious.)*

WILMA. You – you did rap my knuckles.

CAROLINE. Yes, I did. When you deserved it. When you were wrong. When you had to be corrected.

WILMA. I won't let you take them away.

CAROLINE. And what a house that would be if I didn't. Wading, wading, all of you wading –

WILMA. You're not right for them.

CAROLINE. – wading in this tar forever.

WILMA. I'm right.

CAROLINE. It gives you something to do, doesn't it? All this activity? Something to fill your small little days. Well, you know what – no. These children are not a way to distract yourself from how little you've done with your life. They are two fragile kids who have been through a horrible trauma and need our help.

WILMA. I am helping them!

CAROLINE. Yes, you are, you have given them a roof over their heads and warm milk, and a thousand pitiable looks as you turn off the light. But that is not what they need right now.

WILMA. This is where they belong.

CAROLINE. Here? Wilma. You live ten minutes away. Ten minutes away from this.

WILMA. The children don't know you. They've never even visited you.

CAROLINE. They know me. I've been here.

WILMA. When?

CAROLINE. I visited for weeks that one Christmas, when Tom was off in Scotland.

WILMA. They were three!

CAROLINE. I make an impression.

WILMA. Not at three. At three you're just another adult. They don't know you.

CAROLINE. All the better, then. New life, new start.

WILMA. They'll think that they did something wrong, that they're being punished for something.

CAROLINE. By moving to Arizona? Most people would kill for that punishment.

WILMA. Caroline? You live in a nice home, you have a nice husband. That doesn't make you better than me.

CAROLINE. I never said it did.

WILMA. It doesn't make you more important, make your vote count for more.

CAROLINE. This isn't about votes. I am speaking reason. You are speaking nonsense.

WILMA. It's not nonsense!

CAROLINE. What is it, then?!

WILMA. *(losing it)* I don't want them to forget her! They can't forget her! They'll go off with you and you'll buy them new clothes and they'll see the Grand Canyon and they'll get sunburns and they'll live in your palace and swim in your pool and go on trips to Europe and you and Tom will make them call you mommy and daddy and they'll forget, they'll forget, you'll buy them a dog and they'll forget she ever existed.

CAROLINE. They may have to.

WILMA. No. They can't forget that. Her love. They can't.

CAROLINE. They may have to to survive. To move on.

WILMA. That's not survival. That's a…a lobotomy, that's… electric shock treatment –

CAROLINE. So be it.

WILMA. You – you can't mean that.

CAROLINE. Whatever helps them gallop through.

WILMA. You're a monster.

CAROLINE. Me? You won't ever let them grow up.

WILMA. Of course, I – !

CAROLINE. Like some witch in a fairy tale.

WILMA. How dare you – !

CAROLINE. Walking around here, talking to ghosts -

WILMA. She's here!

CAROLINE. Sacrificing their future for your own perverted obsession.

WILMA. Perverted? She was our sister!

CAROLINE. And she is gone.

WILMA. Never. I will tell them bedtime stories of her kindness, I will sound her name each night at grace, I will make our home a shrine.

CAROLINE. You'll seal them in her coffin and sit on the lid.

WILMA. Stop it! Stop it! You – you have no authority to make any decisions for these children. None!

CAROLINE. Really? Is that what it says in the will?

WILMA. No. In the books upstairs.

CAROLINE. What?

WILMA. The ones open on his desk.

CAROLINE. What about them?

WILMA. There were notes written in the margins.

CAROLINE. So? So he scribbled in his books, what does that have to do with – ?

WILMA. It wasn't his writing.

CAROLINE. The children, then. And I still don't see what –

WILMA. Not the children.

CAROLINE. Fine. Whose? Evelyn's?

WILMA. No. Yours.

CAROLINE. Mine? Wilma, don't be ridiculous, why would I – ?

WILMA. Your writing.

CAROLINE. My writing. I wrote in Oliver's books. And what makes you so sure of that?

WILMA. Well. Your initials.

CAROLINE. …oh.

(*Beat.* **CAROLINE** *shrivels up.* **WILMA** *continues, quietly but confidently.*)

WILMA. Would you like me to get them? I could read them to you.

CAROLINE. …no.

WILMA. I could read you what they say.

CAROLINE. No.

He was supposed to erase them.

It was that Christmas visit. He whispered to me every night in the kitchen until I gave in.

WILMA. Caroline.

CAROLINE. He was charming, persistent.

But cold. We'd meet in his study and when we'd finish…when he was done humiliating me…he'd crack open one of his books and whisper passages in my ear, cruel words to make me feel even worse about what we'd done.

I'd write notes in them during the day - initial them like some dumb love-struck kid. The only place I could be sure he'd read them, my pitiful attempt to force myself into his line of vision.

WILMA. But it ended. Tell me it ended.

CAROLINE. *(nodding)* It was the kids. Side by side every morning at breakfast, passing the syrup. When it got so I couldn't look them in the eyes without suffocating… Tom wasn't even back yet from Edinburgh, but… I left early.

WILMA. Did Evelyn know?

CAROLINE. No. You know her, she thought the best of everyone.

I didn't have a gallery opening.

I wanted the service to be…those who truly loved her, who… I didn't want to defile it with my presence.

I've stunned poor Tom, maybe even lost him. He sits silently across from me at dinner, wondering what kind of woman doesn't go to her baby sister's funeral.

Do you forgive me?

WILMA. That doesn't matter.

She would've.

CAROLINE. I don't think so. Not that.

WILMA. …ask her, then. Ask her now.

CAROLINE. What?

WILMA. She's here. In the air. Ask her.

CAROLINE. Wilma.

WILMA. Ask her.

(**CAROLINE** *nods, tries to speak for a moment.*)

CAROLINE. I can't.

WILMA. Try.

(**CAROLINE** *tries to speak again, fails. She rises. She walks to the piano, sits. She plays the piece, every note a plea of forgiveness. She finishes.*)

CAROLINE. Do you think she…?

(**WILMA** *nods.*)

That's some comfort.

Now give me the number.

WILMA. What?

CAROLINE. I told you I wouldn't forget.

WILMA. But there must be a way we can at least hold on to the – *(piano)*

CAROLINE. It's the right thing to do. A gift for the children. Give me the number.

(**WILMA** *opens her purse and hands* **CAROLINE** *a scrap of paper.*)

WILMA. Tell him we'll do something with the walls.

CAROLINE. Of course. Well.

Take care, then.

(**CAROLINE** *grabs her coat.*)

WILMA. What?

CAROLINE. I think there was a flight back tonight I can still catch.

WILMA. You just got here. You haven't even seen the grave.

CAROLINE. You were right, this was better.

(**WILMA** *takes* **CAROLINE**'s *arm.*)

WILMA. What about the children?

CAROLINE. I think it's…probably best for me to leave them be.

WILMA. Are you sure?

CAROLINE. No. But what do I know?

(CAROLINE *turns to go.*)

WILMA. Look for the flames.

CAROLINE. What?

WILMA. From your plane, the window. The bonfire.

CAROLINE. I will.

(CAROLINE *exits.* WILMA *turns back into the room. She closes her eyes, and breathes in the air, saying farewell. She turns to the piano, as if watching Evelyn play.*)

WILMA. That's it…that's it…a little faster…you've got it now…very good…you're going to be wonderful, Evelyn, wonderful.

(*Lights fade to black.*)

ACT THREE

(The living room as before, with one difference: the walls are now covered in salmon paisley wallpaper. It is three in the morning and only the piano light illuminates the room. The sheet music remains on the rack. A woman in her mid-50's, **SARAH***, sits upright on the piano bench, hands in her lap, dressed in a nightgown, intently staring out the window. A moment, then* **JOE***, salt-and-pepper hair, also in his 50's, dressed in pajamas and robe and enters.* **SARAH** *doesn't notice. He stares at her for a while, and then, gently:)*

JOE. You could at least play. A bench full of music.

SARAH. I didn't want to wake you.

JOE. Then you shouldn't have left.

SARAH. Nonsense.

JOE. I'm attuned to you, my dear. Your absence is my alarm clock.

SARAH. I'd think you'd rest more soundly without all my sleep-talking in your ear.

JOE. No, can't sleep without it anymore. Like people who need a radio on, or white noise.

SARAH. White noise? I certainly hope my nocturnal murmurings provide more entertainment than that.

JOE. They do. "Big Piano."

SARAH. "Big Piano."

(They smile at each other for a moment.)

So many memories to choose from. A comfort. They're here now when we think of them. Right here in the room.

JOE. And that's what we'll do. Fill this room with memories, make it our own.

SARAH. I can't wait.

I still see him, that bear.

JOE. *(his hair)* Even through his greying fur?

SARAH. I see him.

JOE. Glad one of us can.

We should get you back to bed.

SARAH. You go. I can't sleep.

JOE. You sure? Busy day tomorrow. Weekend. Papers to read, crosswords to solve, chores to assign.

SARAH. I'm not that bad. The kitchen tile, is all.

JOE. *(smiling)* And the garden?

SARAH. Well, we have to do something with that poor backyard.

JOE. I swear the lawn wasn't like that at the open house.

SARAH. What do you think they – ? Like they burned someone at the stake.

JOE. *(overly dramatic)* Or something.

SARAH. What?

JOE. There's scraps of paper in the ashes. Ghosts of books.

SARAH. Curiouser and curiouser.

JOE. Okay, c'mon up, I'll read you back to sleep.

SARAH. Not yet.

(A moment as **SARAH** *goes back to looking out the window.)*

JOE. I know what you're looking for.

SARAH. Hm?

JOE. I know.

*(**SARAH** stares at him with surprise, fear and defiance.)*

Please. You need your rest.

SARAH. That's not what the doctor said. He said I was fine.

JOE. He didn't say no rest.

SARAH. Improving.

JOE. Yes, he did say that.

SARAH. So I will sit. I will sit in this lovely room that my husband was kind enough to acquire for me. I will sit and admire its every nook.

JOE. Admire it in the morning, honey.

SARAH. The rest of the house, yes. But this – it's a room that likes the dark, don't you think? Some rooms are meant for sunlight, but this one? It waits all day to reveal its true colors.

JOE. You like it?

SARAH. It's perfect. The best surprise of my life.

JOE. Really?

SARAH. All the times we've driven by, looked in this window –

JOE. Our little Sunday ritual –

SARAH. *(the piano)* And now here we are. And here it is.

(She plays a note. It hangs in the air.)

Was all this…?

JOE. What?

SARAH. A going-away present?

JOE. No.

SARAH. That would be just like you. Wasting money on an extravagant, pointless gesture. Putting your life savings into a –

JOE. I don't know what you're –

SARAH. What did the doctor say?

JOE. You heard him. That you were improving.

SARAH. After that. I saw the two of you talking in the hall.

JOE. Just going over prescriptions.

SARAH. And you wouldn't look me in the eye.

JOE. What?

SARAH. The drive home.

JOE. I looked. I always look. Those eyes? Never miss a chance.

SARAH. Hm. You're my bear.

JOE. That's me.

SARAH. Even when you're lying.

(Beat.)

JOE. All right. I'll tell you the truth.

SARAH. Good.

JOE. I wish I'd just bought the bench. Could've saved a lot of money.

SARAH. Joe.

JOE. Well?

SARAH. I play.

JOE. Not enough.

SARAH. Every morning, then. New tradition. I'll accompany your Rice Krispies. Snap, Crackle –

(She plays a phrase of the piece.)

JOE. Keep going.

SARAH. People are sleeping. You can probably hear it through the panes. Neighborhood Watch will pounce on me.

JOE. I doubt the sound carries that far.

SARAH. Oh, I bet it does. I'll become the pariah of the block. Worse than a barking dog. "Somebody take that piano lady to obedience school, shut her up for good."

*(**SARAH** expects a laugh, doesn't get one from a distressed **JOE**.)*

(off his expression) What?

JOE. Nothing. Just not very funny.

SARAH. Ouch.

JOE. Listen, if you're not going to play…

SARAH. What is it?

JOE. It's got to be cold there - the window.

SARAH. I'm fine.

JOE. Well, I – I don't like to…to look at you there. You're always there. Of all the spots in the house.

SARAH. So?

JOE. I think it might be…bad luck. To always sit there.

SARAH. Why, is the couch getting jealous?

JOE. I'm serious. What about…ghosts?

SARAH. Why are you stuck on ghosts all of a sudden?

JOE. I don't know.

SARAH. Getting superstitious in your old age?

JOE. It's just common sense.

SARAH. *(who is this guy?)* Uh-huh.

JOE. So…will you move?

SARAH. Not right now. But don't worry, I'm not as sedentary as you think. When you're away at work, I explore this place, I mount expeditions, solve mysteries.

JOE. You do? And what have you – ?

SARAH. There were children here.

JOE. Children? I don't think so. That's not what the lady said.

SARAH. You're avoiding my eyes again.

JOE. I'm not!

SARAH. I found a pair of dice hidden under the kitchen sink. *(amused)* Under the sink.

JOE. Maybe they had a gambling plumber.

SARAH. Ha ha. Not just that, here and there a toy soldier.

JOE. That's hardly –

SARAH. And – the piece de resistance – in the closet.

JOE. Which?

SARAH. The one in your office?

JOE. What about it? I didn't see –

SARAH. Easy to miss. Way in the back, in the corner, so small.

JOE. Another soldier?

SARAH. No. A drawing. A sweet little drawing.

JOE. Oh. Well, don't worry, I'll paint over it.

SARAH. NO!

No, leave it.

There were two of them.

JOE. Two?

SARAH. *(smiling)* I'll show you the drawing. There were two.

(Her smile grows.)

And you…knew.

That there were two. You knew.

JOE. *(caught)* I… I didn't want to mention it, didn't want to upset you or –

SARAH. No, darling, no, I love it. To feel children in the air. I imagine those two playing upstairs while I wash the dishes, imagine hearing a constant buzz of activity above me while the water runs through my hands –

JOE. I hope it doesn't change how you feel about –

SARAH. It's wonderful. To be in a house where there was that happiness.

Thank you.

JOE. You're welcome.

SARAH. I know your commute is longer.

JOE. It's nothing.

SARAH. It's something. And how you could ever afford -

JOE. They were willing to negotiate.

SARAH. But it had to be –

JOE. A bargain. She was a sweet lady, I merely had to explain the situation: that I had a gorgeous wife who deserved this.

SARAH. *(smiling)* "Big Piano."

JOE. *(returning the smile)* Exactly.

SARAH. You know, I still think you might've made that up.

JOE. Cross my heart. We'd been snooping around here earlier that day, I was having trouble sleeping, lying wide awake all night beside you, listening to your incoherent mumblings. Until, suddenly, crystal clear – "Big Piano" – and a shit-eating grin.

SARAH. Mortifying.

JOE. Are you kidding? I laughed you awake.

SARAH. You're a tolerant man.

JOE. It's easy with such a pretty persecutor.

SARAH. Pretty? God, that's got to be harder to find now than the bear.

JOE. No. It's still there. And I don't even have to squint.

SARAH. Our poor little spinet.

JOE. I'm sure it's found a good home by now.

SARAH. I hope so.

(She looks around the room.)

Just one thing.

JOE. What?

SARAH. It's odd.

JOE. What?

SARAH. The wallpaper. When we'd drive by? I don't remember the wallpaper.

JOE. No?

SARAH. I wonder why they…they had such good taste otherwise.

JOE. Oh.

I'm sorry.

SARAH. It's not your fault.

JOE. I thought you'd like it.

SARAH. Don't take it personally.

JOE. I have to.

I picked it out.

SARAH. What?

JOE. Part of the deal. A fresh... I...thought you'd like it.

SARAH. My bear.

JOE. I thought it was...pretty.

SARAH. And it is. Just maybe not for this room.

JOE. Sure, yeah, I can see that.

SARAH. Let's pick out something together. We could even put it up ourselves – a project – like the Army apartment.

JOE. I'll take care of it.

SARAH. I'm not bedridden.

JOE. I know, but - this was supposed to be a gift.

SARAH. And it is darling, it is.

(They smile.)

JOE. All right, now I'm up.

*(**JOE** turns on a lamp.)*

Can I make you something? Some soup?

SARAH. No.

JOE. Tea? Milk?

SARAH. Milk would be wonderful.

JOE. Hot? Cold?

SARAH. Cold's fine.

*(**JOE** exits, **SARAH**'s eyes following him out of the room. A moment, then as quickly as she can muster, she crosses the room and turns off the lamp **JOE** clicked on, then returns to her perch at the piano bench. She looks out the window, filled with hope and fear. She sees something, smiles with relief mixed with sheer joy. **JOE** re-enters with the milk. He watches **SARAH** for a moment, then –)*

JOE. He's there, isn't he?

*(**SARAH** doesn't answer, caught in the act but not willing to break her gaze.)*

On the corner.

Under the street lamp.

Sitting on his bicycle.

Staring at you.

SARAH. ...how did you know?

JOE. Last night. The bed was empty, I woke up, went to the window, I don't know why. I looked outside, at the street below...and he was there, looking in.

SARAH. Oh.

JOE. For hours. Hours.

SARAH. Yes.

JOE. How many nights has this – ?

SARAH. A week or two.

JOE. A week?!

SARAH. Since we moved in.

JOE. Sweetheart. You need your – !

SARAH. My rest, I know. But I need this more.

JOE. Do you know him?

SARAH. Not at all.

JOE. Then why is he – ?

SARAH. I don't know.

I couldn't sleep and came down here to...to absorb what you'd given me, the enormity of it. I stood in the middle of the dark room and breathed it in, breathed in your generosity, your love. Then I clicked on the piano light and sat down on the bench. I looked out the window – maybe I saw some movement? – and there he was.

Under the street lamp. The boy. Straddling his bicycle. Staring at me in wonder.

And I stared back. Like at an animal, a deer, afraid I would scare him away. His eyes... I didn't know what he wanted.

We sat there, each in our pool of light, with an ocean of darkness between us.

It started off like some odd game of chicken and then became something… *(can't find the words)*

I blinked or nodded off, and he was gone. Vanished. I went back to bed, into your arms. You were sleeping, but your body took me in. It always does.

I woke up not entirely sure it wasn't all a dream.

JOE. But it wasn't.

SARAH. The next night I forced myself to stay awake, padded downstairs at three a.m. He was waiting for me.

JOE. And this has…?

SARAH. Every night since.

JOE. We should talk to him, tell his parents.

SARAH. We are his parents, Joe. Or I'm his mother, at least.

JOE. Sarah, what are you – ?

SARAH. He's come to me. Felt my need.

JOE. He's not your child, sweetheart.

SARAH. For a few hours each night he is. A tiny miracle, but a miracle, all the same.

JOE. A miracle? Some boy sneaking off in the middle of the night to ride his bike, staring into strangers' windows –

SARAH. Not strangers'. Mine.

JOE. You are a stranger to him, Sarah.

SARAH. Not anymore. I'm expected now. Understood. Needed.

JOE. This is crazy.

(**JOE** *moves toward the front door.*)

SARAH. Joe!

JOE. I'll be back in a minute.

SARAH. If you open that door, I'll never speak to you again.

(**JOE** *stops in his tracks, slowly takes his hand off the doorknob.*)

I imagined what our child would look like. Named her, him. Every room we've ever slept in, from the Army apartment till now, I've always placed a baby in a crib.

JOE. Honey.

SARAH. And now I realize how foolish that was. All that time wasted on whether he'd have your eyes or my hair? Pointless. That's not how a mother knows her child. It's deeper than that, more than that. That is my boy. And I know it as certain as I know you are my husband.

JOE. *(wounded)* Really?

How many pills did you take tonight?

SARAH. It's not that.

JOE. The side effects – the label said they might make you -

SARAH. It's not the pills.

JOE. How do you know?

SARAH. Because I didn't take any.

JOE. What?

SARAH. I'm past pills.

JOE. Sweetheart – !

SARAH. I won't spend my last days suffering from side effects.

JOE. Last days? Honey, you're hardly –

SARAH. Last days.

*(A stare-down. **JOE** acquiesces.)*

JOE. But you will spend them there. On that bench.

SARAH. Yes.

JOE. Depriving yourself of sleep, staring out the window at some street urchin.

SARAH. Don't call him that. He has a home.

JOE. This is our home, your home.

SARAH. It's that, too.

JOE. No, this was only for you, to give you something that –

SARAH. A big send-off?

JOE. Peace. I wanted to give you peace.

SARAH. And you have. You gave him to me.

JOE. No.

SARAH. If we hadn't moved –

JOE. No.

SARAH. If there wasn't this piano, if I wasn't sitting in this window –

JOE. Sarah. He's someone else's child. He has a mother somewhere, a real mother.

SARAH. But I make him happy. And he does the same.

JOE. *(wounded)* He makes you happy.

SARAH. Yes.

JOE. You know you keep – you keep putting him on the same plane as –

SARAH. Darling.

JOE. I am your husband.

SARAH. And he is my son.

JOE. No. He is a boy on a bicycle.

SARAH. Don't use that tone with him.

JOE. What tone?

SARAH. This will be a house of love, not anger.

JOE. Honey.

SARAH. That's what I want. And I want you to love him, too.

JOE. Oh, Jesus.

SARAH. More than anything, my bear, I do.

JOE. Maybe we should go to the hospital.

SARAH. Don't you dare.

JOE. Just to let the doctor see you honey, run some more tests.

SARAH. I need to be here.

JOE. *(had enough, slightly mocking)* Here? Why? He'll follow you. Right? Won't he follow you?

SARAH. Don't make fun of me.

JOE. If he's yours? Won't he follow the bread crumbs? Won't you look out the hospital window and see him down there in the parking lot, staring up at you?

SARAH. You've never belittled me before.

JOE. *(repentant but still angry)* I know, I know, but I –

SARAH. You've never made me feel stupid.

JOE. I'm sorry honey, but – !

SARAH. A lifetime of kindness and you mock me now?

JOE. I'm just trying to – let's get a few tests, and – !

SARAH. NO! Why won't you let me have this joy? How can you deny me this joy?!

(They stare at each other for a moment, both furious. **JOE** *leaps into action, crosses to the lamp.)*

Joseph!

*(***JOE*** *clicks the lamp on.)*

Turn that off! I can't see him with -

JOE. Move.

SARAH. Joe?

JOE. Move to the couch.

SARAH. Joseph –

JOE. The couch, the couch!

(She does so reluctantly, leaving the bench.)

SARAH. Please don't do this.

JOE. Sit.

(She does so.)

SARAH. He'll panic without me there, he'll ride away, he'll never come back.

JOE. Good.

SARAH. Was it Jackie Paper or Puff?

JOE. What?

SARAH. Who stopped coming? The song.

JOE. What does this – ?

SARAH. One of them did. I can't do that to him. I can't let him down like that.

JOE. This was a mistake, the house, everything, another mistake. Another failure.

SARAH. Joseph.

JOE. He's killing you! He's taking you away from me!

SARAH. No.

(quiet, knowing this will hurt him) Joe. My time with him…this time. It's the only time the pain fades.

JOE. *(heartbroken)* Don't say that.

SARAH. I'm sorry.

JOE. You can't say that. After everything I've done.

SARAH. I know.

JOE. I wash your feet.

SARAH. And it's lovely. But it doesn't stop the pain.

JOE. Well, why not? WHY NOT?!

(Quiet. A shift in **JOE.***)*

(soft) It goes away? All of it?

SARAH. Yes.

JOE. For hours?

SARAH. As long as he's there.

JOE. I can't accept that.

SARAH. You have to.

JOE. I give you a lifetime, and he just rides in on a bike?

SARAH. It's not a contest. Be happy for me. You've always been happy for me. You've gone to such lengths to – I've never felt worthy of what you've given me.

JOE. But it wasn't enough.

SARAH. Of course it was. Your generosity is dark, bottomless. Albino fish swim down there, strange creatures that don't need light to live.

JOE. You make me sound scary.

SARAH. You are, sometimes. You do scare me. The depths of your generosity.

JOE. Not deep enough.

SARAH. Stop it. Don't ever question what you've given me. My life would be nothing without you.

JOE. It would've had children. Your life. And that clearly –

SARAH. Honey –

JOE. It clearly is enough of a need that *(the boy outside)*… years of smiles and nods and shakes of the head, they were all feints, you were keeping your longing from me, the true depths of your longing. Those were your depths: your need, your longing. You hid them from me, didn't you, hid yourself from me, you must've. Hide and seek from your husband.

SARAH. No.

JOE. And this is where it leads.

SARAH. No.

JOE. The desperation, the longing.

SARAH. Joe.

JOE. To a boy on a bike under a streetlight.

SARAH. Please.

JOE. I did everything I could.

SARAH. I know you did.

JOE. I tried everything.

SARAH. Please, darling.

JOE. To know it's your fault? To know that I was the one denying your happiness, my body was denying you, betraying me, turning an act of pleasure into, into torture and shame and - and you were kind, you were kind, but that smile, that sad smile you'd get staring at little flower girls, that longing in your eyes, I saw that, I saw that every time, every time, and I'd pat you on your knee, and I'd look you in your eyes and I would curse myself, I would curse the death inside me, the useless body that couldn't even get the easy stuff right. I was so happy, so happy, you know that? For us to get older? I prayed for it to hurry up already, bring on the arthritis, the lazy bladder, hurry up, hurry up! Because it meant the end of trying, the end of disappointment, the end of expectation. And then it came. It came and it made me a fool. Because then it was your turn. Time for your body to betray you. In ways I could never have imagined. They conspired against us, our bodies, they were in league to make us miserable.

SARAH. I was never miserable. Whatever life threw at me, all the thousands of disappointments – I had you. Holding my hand.

JOE. Holding you back.

SARAH. Never. Never.

JOE. Don't lie to me, please don't lie.

SARAH. Joe.

JOE. I want to be everything to you, I want to be enough. I want to guide you out of this world, to shepherd you, to see where you've gone so I can follow after.

SARAH. You will. When it's time.

JOE. I won't make it without you. How will I make it without you?

SARAH. You have to. I won't forgive you if you don't.

(**JOE** *manages to return her smile.*)

Promise me something? When I'm gone?

JOE. Anything.

SARAH. I mean it, bear.

JOE. So do I.

SARAH. You'll sell the house. You'll move far away from here. You'll live for yourself.

(*Pause.*)

JOE. I promise.

SARAH. Thank you.

(**JOE***'s face changes.*)

What?

JOE. No.

I can't promise that.

SARAH. You have to.

JOE. No.

SARAH. Why not?

JOE. Because it's not what you really want. Is it?

SARAH. …no.

(**JOE** *takes her hand.*)

JOE. I promise you I will stay here, in this house. And every morning at three a.m. you will sleep-talk in my ear, tell me to wake up. I will come down the stairs and I will sit on the bench and I will look out the window. I will watch the boy. I will watch as he grows taller, as his face lengthens, as a wispy moustache begins to grace his upper lip, as the bicycle becomes a car. I will watch our child grow up. I will bear witness. For you.

(**SARAH** *kisses his hand gratefully.*)

SARAH. On one condition.

JOE. Yes?

SARAH. You keep the wallpaper.

JOE. Why?

SARAH. Because you thought it was pretty.

(**JOE** *nods. He rises. He turns the light switch off, then escorts* **SARAH** *to the bench.* **SARAH**'s *head is down, afraid to look. She gathers herself and then lifts her face, gazing out the window, searching.*)

JOE. Is he still there?

SARAH. *(relief)* Yes.

JOE. Good.

Play something.

(**SARAH** *nods and plays the piece, beautifully.* **JOE** *gazes at* **SARAH**, *she at the boy. Then* **SARAH** *smiles, a satisfied, joyous smile.*)

SARAH. He can hear me.

JOE. How can you tell?

SARAH. He's dancing.

(Lights fade to black.)

End of Play